*To my fourth-graders at Union Elementary School: Dream Big Friends!
And also a big thanks to my rock star friends Jennifer Adcock
and Shiela Johnston for all their support.*

The Garden in My Mind

Growing through Positive Choices

Written by **Stephie McCumbee**

Illustrated by **Lisa M. Griffin**

BOYS TOWN
Press

Boys Town, Nebraska

The Garden in My Mind
Text and Illustrations Copyright © 2014, by Father Flanagan's Boys' Home
ISBN 978-1-934490-54-9

Published by the Boys Town Press
14100 Crawford St.
Boys Town, NE 68010

For a Boys Town Press catalog, call **1-800-282-6657**
or visit our website: **BoysTownPress.org**

Publisher's Cataloging-in-Publication Data

McCumbee, Stephie.

The garden in my mind : growing through positive choices / written by Stephie McCumbee ;
illustrated by Lisa M. Griffin. – Boys Town, NE : Boys Town Press, c2014.

    p. : ill. ; cm.

    ISBN: 978-1-934490-54-9
    Audience: Grades 1-6.

    Summary: Using a garden metaphor, the author explains how to ignore distractions, take
responsibility for your behaviors and make better choices. This richly illustrated picture book
offers valuable life lessons to young readers so they can "grow their garden" in school and at
home.–Publisher.

    1. Children–Life skills guides–Juvenile literature. 2. Social skills in children–Juvenile
literature. 3. Attention in children–Juvenile literature. 4. Distraction (Psychology)–Juvenile
literature. 5. Responsibility in children–Juvenile literature. 6. Decision making in children–Juvenile literature. 7. [Conduct of life. 8. Social skills. 9. Attention. 10. Responsibility. 11. Decision
making.] I. Griffin, Lisa M. (Lisa Middleton), 1972- II. Title.

HQ783 .M33 2014

303.3/2–dc23   1402

Printed in the United States
10 9 8 7 6 5 4 3 2 1

Boys Town Press is the publishing division of Boys Town,
a national organization serving children and families.

Yesterday, Trey Thompson and I were making spitballs when "Little Miss Perfect Shaina" looked at us, cocked her head, and shook it. "That Shaina gets on my ever-loving nerves," I said. Then we started to sing,

"Shaina Baina BO Baina Me My Mo Maina."

Suddenly, Mrs. Julian stopped in mid-sentence and gave us The Eye. I knew we were in for it then! "I need to speak with the two of you in the hall please," Mrs. Julian said. I felt everyone staring at me as I walked toward the door.

When Mrs. Julian came out of the room, she said, "Grass withers and flowers fade every time a bad choice is made." Trey scrunched his eyebrows and asked, "What in the world is that supposed to mean?"

"It's like this," she said. "Your brain is like a sponge. It has many flower seeds just waiting to grow. Each time you are doing your best, you are watering your seeds.

Each time you make a bad choice, your flowers begin to fade. It's time you start to think about your choices and how they may be hurting you."

I heard what Mrs. Julian said loud and clear. The problem was, I wanted to make good choices. I really did. But I wasn't sure I knew hOw. When she let us back in the class, I returned to my spot on the floor. Finally, the bell rang.

I was not sure if Mrs. Julian was telling the truth or not, but I started to think about what would happen if she was right. Sometimes I guess I just don't stop and think. At least that's what my mom told me.

Soon, my mom pulled up.

When I saw her, she asked me how my
day was. "Horrible, just terrible," I said.
I told her all about getting called out of
class and what Mrs. Julian had said.

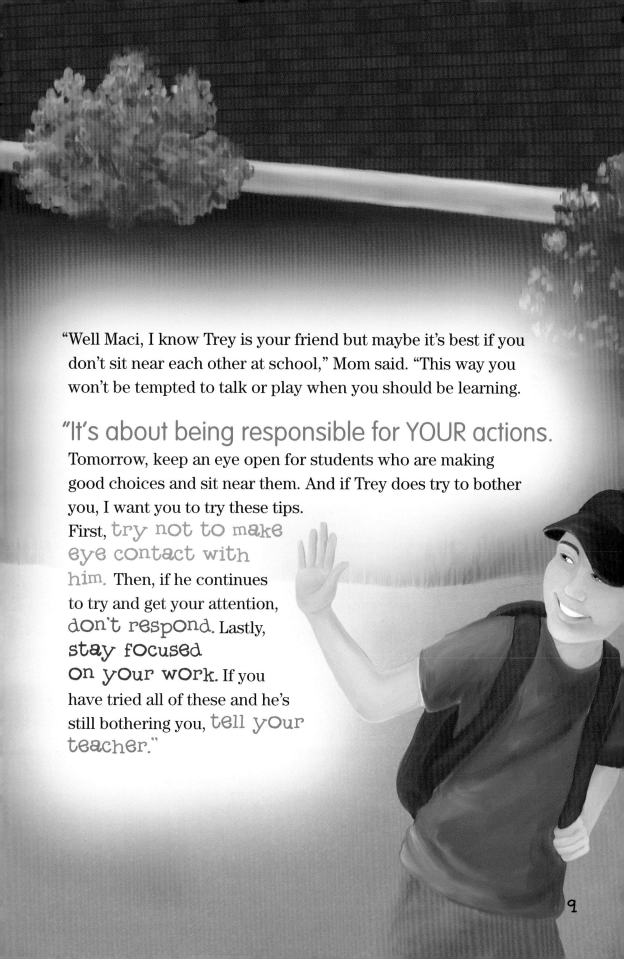

"Well Maci, I know Trey is your friend but maybe it's best if you don't sit near each other at school," Mom said. "This way you won't be tempted to talk or play when you should be learning.

"It's about being responsible for YOUR actions. Tomorrow, keep an eye open for students who are making good choices and sit near them. And if Trey does try to bother you, I want you to try these tips. First, try not to make eye contact with him. Then, if he continues to try and get your attention, don't respond. Lastly, stay focused on your work. If you have tried all of these and he's still bothering you, tell your teacher."

the room started to spin

On the way to class the next morning,
I thought about what my mom had told me.
Suddenly, the hallway seemed strange.
When I opened the classroom door,

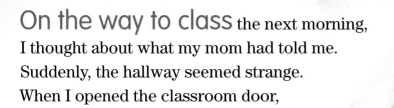

like one of those teacup rides at the state fair.

Before long, it stopped, and every person in the room had a big yellow sponge floating on the very top of their head! The sponges were like the kind my dad uses to wash the car. Some students' sponges had thick gardens filled with beautiful wild flowers, while other students' sponges looked dry and dead.

"Little Miss Perfect Shaina's" sponge
was packed with flowers. It looked like she
was wearing my Aunt TeTe's
Chia Pet on her head!
She is always making good
choices. I should probably
sit near her, I thought.

I walked over to where Shaina
was sitting, pushing her big flowers out
of the way. I took a seat.

When class started, Trey tried to change seats with Ryeleigh Jane so we could sit together. I pictured little grub worms eating my flowers and decided to give tip number one a shot.

"Don't make eye contact," I said to myself. I turned my back to him. It worked!

16

During silent reading time,
Shaina read in the Book Nook.
When Trey made hissing sounds
to get her attention, she
never even looked up!
She was ignoring him just
like Mom had told me to do!

Shaina's flowers began to sprout.
I couldn't believe how easy it was to make better choices.
I picked up my book and sat beside Shaina on the couch.
Tip number two had worked for Shaina.

During writers' workshop, Mrs. Julian asked the class to write about a time when they were scared. I didn't even know where to start!

Trey was busy creating ninja stars. He shot one across the room and hit Hunter Lane right between the eyes!

I looked over at Shaina
and she was making a list.

"stay
focused,"

I thought.

21

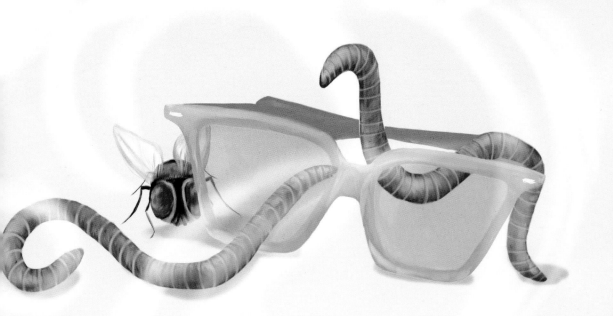

I grabbed a pencil and started making a list, too. I felt my sponge tingle. My mom would be so proud of me. Tip number three was pretty easy! Mrs. Julian asked Trey to share what he was afraid of. He stood up real tall and said,

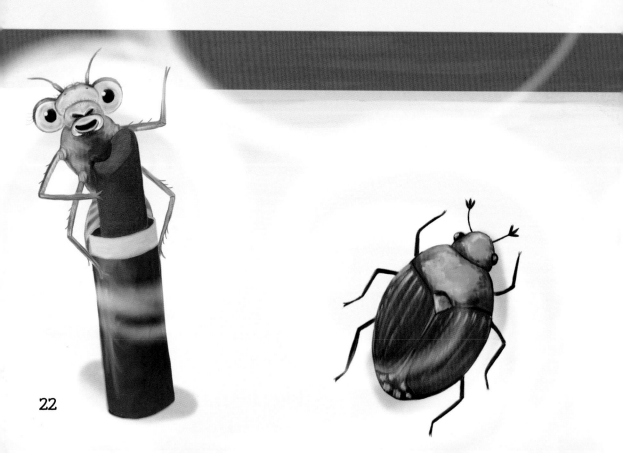

"Poisonous
bugs
and
girly hugs."

Mrs. Julian was
not amused.

23

24

After lunch, Mrs. Julian read the class a story. Shaina listened closely while Trey sprawled out on the carpet – belly first, like one of those polar bear rugs I've seen on TV. I'm pretty sure he was sleeping.

Mrs. Julian finished the story and asked the class to write a summary. Trey used his eraser caps to build an imaginary army. He asked me to play, but I ignored him and began writing. Something different was happening right away.

I felt little **flowers** popping up on my sponge.

It wasn't long until I had finished and was able to go to recess. Trey had to stay inside and finish his work.

Pretty soon it was time for science.
Mrs. Julian told us to pick a partner. I couldn't
believe my luck when Shaina picked
*ME!

Suddenly, I heard loud hooting sounds from across the room. It was Trey, hooting like an owl with Oreo cookies covering his eyes. Everyone in the class started to laugh except Shaina and me. I was getting good at ignoring Trey. I could tell Mrs. Julian was upset. I began to feel bad about all the times I had disrupted the class.

At last, it was the end of the day.

While everyone was lining up, Mrs. Julian called me over to her desk. "Maci, you have been a great gardener today," she said. "I love the way you stayed focused on your work and didn't distract others. You're one day closer to a blossoming garden." Then, she raised her hand in the air and gave me a great big high-five. I couldn't wait to tell Mom the good news!

31

I looked over at my new friend Shaina; her big spongy garden hat with all the flowers had disappeared.

I don't know what happened that day, but I was really glad it did. My brain helped me see choices as they happened in a way I will never forget!

I even felt a little sorry for Trey.
He couldn't see how his choices were hurting him.
Luckily for him, I know about the secret tips.

Tomorrow I plan to tell him all about them.

On the way home, we passed by a field of wild flowers and I thought more about my day. I decided to ask Trey if he would like to grow a garden with me.

Mom would sure be proud of me.

Gardening 101

Maci's Tips

Give your full attention to the task you are doing.

Refocus yourself if distractions are brewing.

Observe "gardeners" whose good choices help their gardens grow.

Work together to create your best flower show.

Tips for Educators and Parents

❋ **Reward children** who are exhibiting positive choices. This will help to refocus those who might not be making good choices.

❋ Make **learning social skills** authentic. Help students see how making positive choices relates to their world.

❋ **Verbally praise** children when they make positive choices.

❋ **Use proactive teaching** instead of reactive teaching. Teach children how to behave in situations before they encounter them. This reduces the chances that students will make negative choices.

✳ Help youngsters avoid situations that might encourage negative choices.

✳ Role-play what positive and negative choices look like in new situations. For example, if you are planning to allow children to complete a new activity, show them how they should behave (proactive).

✳ Build respect and trust. Having an open line of communication will help you redirect a student who may not be making positive choices.

✳ Begin the school year by limiting opportunities for negative behavior as you teach positive behavior skills that can give children more freedom.

✳ Promote frequent parent-teacher communication; this is vital to monitoring students' success.